MAIDSTONE

13/7/~

Please return on or before the latest date above.
You can renew online at www.kent.gov.uk/libs
or by phone 08458 247 200

MAI
Needs

ot
lesmaid

e Wilkins

mela Venus

823.914   FAMILY ISSUES —
            HEALTH/DISABILITY

CUSTOMER SERVICE EXCELLENCE   Libraries & Archives   Kent County Council

ind

Text © 2003 Verna Allette Wilkins
Illustrations © 1995 Pamela Venus

Published 1995; Reprinted 2003; This edition 2005
ISBN 1 870516 30 3

C152851894

KT-445-062

Nicky was at the back of her house playing cricket with Jason from next door and Rashid from number 12.

They were both brilliant cricketers.

The game was getting frantic.

Out of the corner of one eye, Nicky saw her favourite Aunt walking towards the house.

"Hi! Auntie Flora," she gasped, just as Jason whacked the ball. "Mum's indoors."

"Hi Nicky, will you come in, too?" asked Aunt Flora.

"Not yet! In a sec… Rashid, catch!"

"Jason, you're out at last!" yelled Rashid as he grabbed the flying ball.

1

A little while later her mother's voice called from the open door. "Nicky! Nicky! Come here."

"Oh no!" Nicky groaned.

She hated it when her mother interrupted a brilliant game. She was just about to go in to bat.

"Hang on a minute!" she said to Jason and Rashid as she galloped into the house.

Her mother and Aunt Flora were in the kitchen looking through glossy magazines.

Nicky hoped they weren't choosing dresses for her. She hated dresses and fussy, frilly clothes.

"Nicky," said her mother, "Auntie Flora is getting married next month, and she would like to ask you a very special favour."

Nicky tapped one foot on the kitchen floor. Her mother was wearing her 'please be good' look. But Nicky just wanted to get back to the cricket.

"I would like you to be one of my bridesmaids," said Aunt Flora quickly.

Nicky loved her Aunt Flora, but all the bridesmaids she had ever seen wore fussy, frilly dresses with ribbons and bows. Even worse, they wore fancy, satiny shoes. But worst of all, if she stayed indoors any longer, Rashid would take her place and go in to bat.

"Will I have to wear a fussy, frilly dress with ribbons and bows?" she asked.

"Just one frill, but no ribbons or bows," promised Aunt Flora.

"Well... All right then... Oh! Aunt Flora... Can I wear boots?" asked Nicky.

"What?" gasped her mother. "Boots on a bridesmaid?"

"Well... Maybe..." said Aunt Flora, but she looked very worried.

"I'm going to look really silly! Even one fussy frill is awful!" thought Nicky, as she raced back to the game.

She was so busy making up horrid pictures in her head of herself wearing a silly, frilly dress, that she crashed into a huge, flowering plant. It ruined the rest of her game. Nicky had hay fever.

That evening, Nicky asked her mum, "How will I carry my bridesmaid's flowers? If I keep sneezing in church, I'll ruin everything. I'll have runny eyes and a runny nose just like this. I can't be a bridesmaid! I can't!"

"Oh yes, you can. We'll think of something," said her mum. "When I was a little girl, I really wanted to be a bridesmaid. My best friend got chosen more than once, but nobody wanted me to be their bridesmaid. You're a lucky girl, Nicky!"

"But what's so great about being a bridesmaid if you don't want to be one anyway!" Nicky moaned.

"Come on, Nicky. Auntie Flora chose you because you're special."

"But I hate dresses!"

"But Nicky," said Mum, gently, "you've been going on about new boots for ages. Now's your chance to choose a great pair."

Next morning, on the way to school, Nicky wouldn't even smile at her mum's jokes.

"Come on, Nicky!" said Mum. "You'll be a beautiful bridesmaid."

"I could never be beautiful in a silly, frilly dress, Mum," said Nicky. "You know that."

"But Nicky, remember the boots!" said Mum. "The wedding will be fun and won't even last all day. The boots will be fun and last for ages! That's if you don't wear them to play cricket!"

They both giggled.

"Better now?" asked Mum.

"Think so," said Nicky, and dashed off to meet up with her school friends.

At school, her best friend Maisie ignored her and talked to some of the other children instead. "No one's ever asked me to be a bridesmaid," moaned Maisie, "but Nicky can't stop complaining."

"Maybe she's just showing off," said Joanna.

"I know how she feels," said Tim. "I hated it when I had to dress up in a funny suit with a frilly shirt and velvet trousers for my big sister's wedding."

"But," said Maisie, "did Nicky tell you about the boots? She's wearing boots to the wedding!"

"Boots on a bridesmaid?" said Tim and Joanna together.

They all giggled and ran off.

Nicky was miserable.

Nobody seemed to understand.

"I won't do it!" she yelled. "I won't. I'll look silly. I shouldn't have promised anything to anybody."

After school, she couldn't find Jason and Rashid.

"There isn't anyone to play with," moaned Nicky. "Only Tig, and she can't play cricket."

"Come here," said Mum. "Dad bought you a beautiful book today. It'll cheer you up."

"What's it called?" asked Nicky.

"*Zaahida's Magic Red Boots*. Come indoors and we'll read it together."

They went indoors and sat down.

When they had finished, Nicky said, "That was good, Mum. It's the best book I've ever read. I'll have red boots for the wedding!"

"I agree," said Mum.

"Is the dress ready yet?" Nicky asked.

"Not yet," said her mum. "Tomorrow I want you to try it on to check if the size is right."

The first fitting of the dress was horrid.

It was all in bits. It looked awful and felt itchy.

"Keep still," said Mum.

"Ouch!" cried Nicky. A stray pin jabbed her tummy when she turned to shoo Rashid and Jason away from the window.

They were laughing and pulling faces.

Jason called out, "Nicky, you look like a scarecrow."

"Mum," groaned Nicky, "do I really look like a scarecrow?"

"Of course not. You're beautiful," said her mum and tickled her chin. "You wait and see," said Mum.

"You'll be the most wonderful bridesmaid ever."

Nicky wasn't so sure.

Nicky's mum spent many days working on the dress.

One night, Nicky crept downstairs for a drink.

It was nearly midnight and her mum was still sewing.

"It's very late, Mum. Haven't you finished yet?" asked Nicky.

"Oh, I've got loads more to do," her mother replied.

"I hope Mum's not adding another pile of frills to my dress and hoping I won't notice," thought Nicky, as she trotted back to bed.

At last, the dress was finished. The dreaded frill was on. Rashid and Jason crept back to the window, hoping to get some more laughs.

"Gosh!" gasped Rashid. "She looks like an angel!" They could hardly believe their eyes.

Nicky, champion cricketer, was wearing a beautiful, long dress. And she looked great.

18

Jason was speechless for once.

But Nicky couldn't wait to change into trousers and get back to her cricket.

The cricket team had played and won a series of games. They made it to the championship finals and won.

Nicky raced home with her good news.

"Brilliant! You deserved to win. You all worked really hard for it," said her mum.

But she too was soon back at work and the sewing machine whizzed and whirred on and on.

T hen one Saturday morning, Nicky, Mum and Aunt Flora went on a shopping trip to find the red boots.

Every shop assistant they spoke to said, "Boots for a bridesmaid? Not really. Try these," and showed them dainty, satiny shoes instead.

They travelled up and down the High Street. They went in and out of umpteen shops. There were no red boots to be found anywhere.

They were just about to give up when Nicky spotted some in a shop window.

"Mum! Auntie Flora!" she called excitedly. "Look. I've found them. These are the ones!"

"Oh yes!" said her mum. "They are lovely.
I think I shall have a pair too." She bought a pair,
exactly the same as Nicky's.

Nicky wondered.

She and Mum never wore identical shoes or identical
anything.

"Only twins do that," she thought.

Nicky was happy for a while until
she remembered her hay fever.

Carrying flowers would make her nose run.
She would sneeze and sneeze and sneeze.

She had nightmares about it.

In her worst dreams, she sneezed away
the bride's veil, and made her Gran scatter
confetti all over the guests inside
the church.

Everyone turned to stare.

The nightmares were
terrible.

23

Then, at last, the big day arrived. It was warm and sunny. A real hay feverish kind of day. Nicky started to worry all over again.

Just after breakfast, Granny Belper arrived in a very bright outfit, covered in flowers.

Nicky nearly sneezed just looking at the flowery dress.

Suddenly the house seemed full of people.

"Come on, dearie," said Gran, bustling in. "Let me help you to get dressed. Here, have this," she said, giving Nicky a peppermint, and a ringlet of flowers.

Nicky held them away from her. "I'll sneeze my head off if I put these in my hair!" She held her breath, waiting for the dreaded sneezing to begin.

"Where's Mum?" Nicky wondered. "Why is Gran here and not Mum?"

Her mother had disappeared.

24

Just as a big car arrived to take the guests to the church, Mum appeared.

"Oh Mum!" said Nicky. "Now I know why you were so busy. And you're a bridesmaid at last… You look really great."

"And so do you, Nicky," smiled Mum. "Don't worry about the flowers in your hair. And you can hold the bouquet as close as you like. It's made of silk."

"Did you make the flowers as well?" asked Nicky.

Mum nodded and smiled.

"Thanks Mum. You're ace!"

Just then, Tig jumped onto the path.

"Great," said Mum. "Black cats are said to be lucky at weddings. Let's go."

Aunt Flora's wedding was fun. Gran Belper sang out loud and out of tune. Nicky didn't sneeze once. There was fabulous food at the party afterwards.

"I've got a tummy ache," groaned Jason.

"Why did you have four helpings of food, then?" laughed Rashid. "Come on Nicky, let's dance!" he said. "Your Auntie Flora's music is great."

"OK," said Nicky, happily.

"I'm much better at cricket than I am at this!" whispered Rashid.

"Ouch!" whispered Nicky. "I think so too."

Why is Nicky's mum in a wheelchair?

Her spinal cord was injured in an accident.

The spinal cord works like a telephone cable sending messages of movement and feeling to the brain. If the spinal cord is injured, these messages can't get through. The result is paralysis below the level of the injury. Most people will need to use a wheelchair as a result of spinal cord injury.

The Spinal Injuries Association is the national charity for people with spinal cord injuries. We offer support, information and advice to individuals and families on all aspects of living with spinal cord injury. Run by paralysed people, over eleven services are available, including a range of publications to help people return to a full life after injury.

We believe it is important that all children have a positive image of family life and disability and we are delighted to publish this book with *Tamarind* for the benefit of all young readers.

Spinal Injuries Association
Newpoint House
76 St James's Lane
London N10 3DF
Telephone: 020 8444 2121

SPINAL INJURIES ASSOCIATION
moving forward after paralysis